101 BUMS

Written by Sam Harper • Illustrated by Chris Jevons

Hodder
Children's
Books

Big bum,

little bum,

scruffy bum,

fluffy bum.

Fast bum,

slow bum,

TAXI

TURTLE TAXI

Mucky bum,

clucky bum,

laying eggs for tea.

Fuzzy bum,

buzzy bum,

what a busy bee!

Prickly bum,

tickly bum.

Ouch, that's very sharp!

Grumpy bum,

stumpy bum.

Watch out! Rumble...

PARP!

Bums in the jungle,

bums in the town.

Bums in the
treetops,
hanging
upside down.

Bums in the farmyard,

bums in the park.

Lots of teeny-tiny bums,
glowing in the dark.

These bums love to **wiggle**.

And those bums like to **jiggle**.

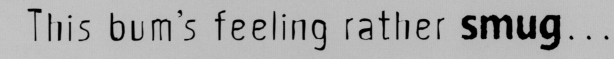

and this bum's **comfy** on the rug.

Some bums are rather **crazy**,

some are very **lazy**,

and this
one's very,
very, very
tall.

Chunky bums,

funky bums,
bopping in the sun.

Jazzy bums,

snazzy bums.

Get set ... ready ... pose!

Pink bum,

Spot bum, **dot** bum, **whiff** bum, **sniff** bum.

Dig bum, **big** bum, **stick** bum, **quick** bum…

Fluffy, scruffy, spotty, dotty,

chunky, funky, small . . .

It's time to shake your botty
at the jiggly wiggly ball!

There are **101** brilliant bums in this book! How many did you spot?

For my family
C.J.

HODDER CHILDREN'S BOOKS

First published in Great Britain in 2020
by Hodder and Stoughton

© Hachette Children's Group, 2020
Illustrations by Chris Jevons

A CIP catalogue record for this book is
available from the British Library.

ISBN: 978 1 44449 500 2

1 3 5 7 9 10 8 6 4 2

Printed and bound in China

FSC
www.fsc.org

MIX
Paper from
responsible sources
FSC® C104740

Hodder Children's Books
An imprint of Hachette Children's Group
Part of Hodder and Stoughton
Carmelite House, 50 Victoria Embankment, London, EC4Y 0DZ

An Hachette UK Company
www.hachette.co.uk
www.hachettechildrens.co.uk